A Young Consumer's Guide

Smart Spending

Lois Schmitt

Thomaston Center School

CHARLES SCRIBNER'S SONS • NEW YORK

Charles Scribner's Sons Books for Young Readers
Macmillan Publishing Company
866 Third Avenue, New York, NY 10022
Collier Macmillan Canada, Inc.

Printed in the United States of America
First Edition   10 9 8 7 6 5 4 3 2 1

Library of Congress Cataloging-in-Publication Data
Schmitt, Lois.
Smart spending: a young consumer's guide / Lois Schmitt.—1st ed.
p.   cm.
Summary: Offers advice on how to recognize and avoid consumer traps. Case studies discuss misleading advertising, consumer fraud, mail-order problems, refund policies, product safety, food poisoning, fad diets, money management, and effective complaining.
1. Consumer education—Juvenile literature.
[1. Consumer education.] I. Title.
TX335.S295   1989
640.73—dc 19   88–29524 CIP AC   ISBN 0–684–19035–4

Contents

CONTENTS

Foreword

A record club delivers the wrong album. Designer jeans purchased at a flea market turn out to be counterfeit. A radio breaks down two weeks after the warranty expires.

Do these situations sound familiar? Chances are, you've faced similar consumer problems. Unless your surname is Trump or Rockefeller, you can't buy everything you want. This means you must get the most satisfaction from the money you have. To do this, you must avoid throwing cash away on merchandise that falls apart shortly after purchase, bears no resemblance to its ad, or is never delivered. In short, you can't afford to be ripped off.

In *Smart Spending,* you will discover how to recognize and avoid consumer traps. This book consists of case studies based on typical problems that you and your friends could face now or during the next few years. Each case is followed by a look at what happened, why it happened, and how it could be avoided.

Think about all the money you spend. Are you usually satisfied with your purchases or do you sometimes wish you had spent your money in some other way? You already are an active consumer. The information in this book will help you become a smart one, too. Read it, enjoy it, and use it.

Smart Spending

1

PROMISES, PROMISES
A Look at Advertising

Every day, you are bombarded with advertisements trying to sell you something. Advertisers try to reach you through TV, radio, neon signs, billboards, window displays, newspapers, and magazines. Advertising is one of the primary devices that a business can use to attract customers, and it does perform a useful service. It tells you what is available and at what cost. By giving you facts about a product, advertising enables you to comparison

1

shop at home. Advertising can be tricky, however, and it could convince you to buy poor-quality merchandise or products you don't need.

CASE A

BAIT AND SWITCH

Jeff was reading the Saturday newspaper when he came across a full-page ad for a bicycle on sale. Jeff had hoped to buy a bike with the money he earned mowing lawns after school. He also wanted to use some of this money to buy a school jacket. Since the bike in the ad cost about the amount Jeff wanted to spend, he decided to go to the store and have a look at it.

When he arrived at the store, Jeff was greeted by Mrs. Wilcox, the sales manager. Jeff asked to see the bike advertised in the newspaper. Mrs. Wilcox immediately pointed out some of the less-attractive features of the advertised model and told Jeff that she hoped he had better taste than to buy "cheap merchandise." She then suggested another model and showed him a bike at a much higher price.

When Jeff insisted that he still wanted the sale model, Mrs. Wilcox told him that they were temporarily out of stock on that item. She added that it would be several weeks before a new shipment would arrive. She continued to

---

emphasize the special features on the more expensive model and pressed hard for a sale. Finally Jeff agreed to buy the higher-priced bike.

When Jeff got home, he began to wonder if he had done the right thing. The special features on the expensive model were not that important to him. And he hadn't wanted to spend that much money. Now he wouldn't be able to buy a school jacket. He began to think that maybe he should have insisted on the sale bike or taken his business elsewhere.

Jeff was the victim of a common advertising trick known as "bait and switch." Mrs. Wilcox had no intention of selling the advertised sale bike. That was merely the "bait" to lure customers into the store. Once they were there, she would try to "switch" them over to a higher-priced model.

Although "bait and switch" tactics are usually associated with "big ticket" items, such as bikes, VCRs, computers, and TVs, this technique is also used during sales for sneakers, jeans, cosmetics, and other less-expensive merchandise. You can recognize "bait and switch" by the following:

• The salesperson belittles the sales merchandise, often saying that you deserve better.

• Even though you insist you want the sale item, the seller persists in trying to convince you to buy a higher-priced model.

• The store is out of stock on the sale merchandise.

If the sale merchandise is what you want, insist on it. If the sales clerk claims that the item is out of stock, ask for a raincheck. A raincheck permits you to buy the item at the sale price when a new shipment is received.

If you live in one of the many states, counties, or cities that have laws requiring stores to make advertised sale merchandise available, you should report any problem to your local consumer affairs agency. Consumer agencies that handle individual complaints can intercede with the store on your behalf and can crack down on frequent offenders.

CASE B

THE BLITZ CAMPAIGN

When Tina asked her brother, Billy, what he wanted for his birthday, he replied that he wanted a "Glampf." This was a new toy on the market that was the rage at Billy's school. "Glampfs" were six-inch-high ceramic figures that had monster faces and purple hair. TV and magazines were filled with ads for this new toy. You could even buy "Glampf" emblems to put on T-shirts.

When Tina went to buy the "Glampf" for her brother, she was disappointed at what she saw. She thought the toy was poorly made

---

and not at all worth the price. She really wanted to get Billy something else for his birthday, but since a "Glampf" was what he wanted, she decided to get it for him.

Billy was delighted with the "Glampf." For the next few days, he took it everywhere with him. By the end of the week, however, Tina noticed that it was just sitting in a corner of the room. When she asked Billy about this, he replied that now that he had the "Glampf," he saw that there really wasn't much you could do with it.

Billy was the victim of a slick advertising campaign. Through TV and magazine advertising, the manufacturer of "Glampfs" created a desire for them. Billy and his friends wanted them for no other reason than that "Glampfs" were everywhere. Each year, particularly around the holiday buying season, the market is flooded with products that advertisers have designated as "in" things. Before buying such an item, ask yourself if you would want it if it weren't so popular.

CASE C

THE TESTIMONIAL

Alan couldn't wait to go ice skating on Saturday and try out his brand-new pair of skates.

The skates were expensive, but he was sure they were worth it. They were the most popular brand on the market. On the sides of the skates was the signature of a famous hockey star. Alan had seen him praising the skates in magazine ads and on TV, so he knew this had to be a top-quality product.

Alan's cousin Michele had new skates, too, but they were an unknown brand. Michele bought them because they were less expensive than the brand that Alan had. Alan was sure Michele would have trouble skating with such a cheap product.

By the time winter ended, Alan wasn't so smug. Michele was perfectly satisfied with her skates, but Alan hadn't been that lucky with his. They were uncomfortable and were coming apart. The manager of the local ice rink told Alan that they were not made as well as some other brands. Alan didn't understand this. Not only were these the most popular skates you could buy, they were advertised by a famous hockey player. Surely a hockey champion wouldn't use skates that were poorly made.

True, a hockey champion would not use skates of poor quality. But he might very well advertise them. Each year, manufacturers spend millions of dollars in payments to movie stars, athletes, and other celebrities for their endorsement of a product. This type of advertising is called a celebrity testimonial, and it's one of the most common types of advertising used. When you see a testimonial ad, don't assume that the celebrity likes or even uses the product. He is appearing in the ad because he is being paid—and paid well—to do so.

CASE D

PHOTOGRAPHIC TECHNIQUES

Kristy wanted to lose weight. She was always going on a diet, but it never seemed to do much good. Dieting was hard, and Kristy loved to eat. One day, while glancing through a magazine, she saw an ad for diet pills. The ad didn't promise a specific weight loss, but it showed "before" and "after" photos of a woman who had used these pills for four weeks. Kristy thought the woman looked as if she had lost more than twenty pounds. The ad said the pills could be purchased at any pharmacy, so Kristy hurried to her local drug store and bought some. Although she took the pills every day for a month, she lost only three pounds.

Kristy was angry. If the diet pills worked for the woman in the advertisement, why didn't they work for her? She mentioned this to her older brother, Michael. Since Michael's hobby was photography, he realized what had happened as soon as he saw the pictures in the

---

ad. Clever photography made the woman in the photos *appear* to have lost weight. Michael pointed out that the "before" picture was taken full face, while the "after" photo was shot at a side angle, to make her look thinner. In the "before" picture, the woman was wearing a light-colored dress with horizontal stripes. This increased the appearance of her size. In the "after" photo, the woman was slimmed down by a solid black dress with a long white tie hanging down the front.

Unfortunately, what you see in an ad is not always what you get. Photographs often make products look more appealing than they actually are. By using certain angles and lighting, a professional photographer can make an object look larger or smaller, fatter or thinner, or brighter or darker than it is. On TV, the use of photography and sound effects can make items appear to move faster and jump higher than they really do. Don't be deceived by a photo in an ad or a picture on your TV screen. Whoever said "pictures don't lie" never knew a good photographer.

CASE E

PUFFING ADS

Fran wasn't satisfied with her hair. There was nothing really wrong with it, but it wasn't

---

spectacular-looking, either. She thought her hair looked dull. One night she saw a TV ad for a new shampoo called Rosebud. The commercial showed a gorgeous woman with long flowing blond hair. Behind her stood a handsome man who held a bottle of shampoo in his hand and said, "Rosebud is the shampoo used by beautiful women." Fran decided that Rosebud might be the solution to her hair problem. The next day she bought a bottle of it and used it on her hair. To her dismay, her hair looked no different than it did when she washed it with her old brand of shampoo.

If Fran had listened carefully to the TV commercial, she would have realized that it never promised hair as lovely as the model's hair in the ad. The Rosebud shampoo commercial was a puffing ad. Puffing ads don't lie; they just don't give you any real information. They use empty claims or create images instead of providing facts. Puffing ads generally use one or more of the following techniques:

• *Transfer.* This technique tries to associate an image with a product. The Rosebud commercial created the image of a beautiful woman and tried to give the impression that if you used this shampoo you'd be beautiful, too. By creating an image, an ad will make you think that you'll be happier, healthier, or more popular if you use a certain product.

• *Glittering generality*. An ad using this technique makes a vague claim without giving any facts to back it up. It may tell you that "Nibbers is the best candy bar you can buy." You're not told why this candy is best; you're expected to take the advertiser's word for it.

• *Association*. This is based on the belief that pleasant associations with a product will cause you to buy it. Breathtaking landscapes, cuddly puppies and kittens, romantic settings, and lively music are used to make you feel good about a product. The better you feel about an item, the more likely you are to buy it.

• *Jingles and slogans*. This technique helps you to remember a product's name. The theory behind using constantly repeated jingles and slogans is that, if a brand name is heard often enough, a feeling of familiarity will be created. For example, if you see several brands of toothpaste on a store shelf, chances are you will take the same brand each time you buy toothpaste. Your choice is based on being familiar with that name, not because it's the best on the market. Catchy jingles and slogans can turn little-known brands into household words.

• *Conformity*. This technique plays on your desire to be part of the group. It's based on the idea that you will use a particular product because it's the popular thing to do. "Our product has helped millions." "We sell more sneakers than anyone." "Everybody is buying Zola Cola." The advertiser hopes you'll buy the merchandise because you want to be like everyone else.

• *Emotional appeal.* The emotion involved can be anger, love, fear, or happiness. "Don't be embarrassed by bad breath." "The perfume to wear when you're with someone you love." These are intended to reach your emotions. Advertisers think that if your emotions are aroused you'll be less likely to look for hard facts about the product.

CASE F

MISLEADING ADS

When Jackie made the school track team, she became interested in keeping her body in good condition. Her coach stressed the importance of rest, exercise, and eating the right foods. One evening, while watching TV, Jackie saw a commercial for a new brand of cereal called Powerhouse. The ad said:

NO OTHER CEREAL HAS MORE
VITAMINS THAN POWERHOUSE.

Since Jackie thought that this brand would be good for her, she asked her mother to buy it. Powerhouse turned out to be twice the price of the brand of cereal Jackie usually had for breakfast, but it didn't taste any better. Still, Jackie wanted her family to continue to buy this new brand because it was so rich in vitamins.

A few weeks later, Jackie compared the vitamin listing on a box of Powerhouse with the ones on several other brands of cereal. To her surprise, they all had exactly the same amounts. The next day, Jackie heard the Powerhouse commercial again. This time, she listened to it carefully. Although the ad gave the impression that Powerhouse was more nutritious than other brands, it never specifically said so.

Jackie was the victim of a misleading ad. The commercial made the viewer *think* that Powerhouse had more vitamins than any other cereal, but that is not what it said. It said that no other cereal had *more* vitamins. That statement was true. Powerhouse and the other cereals on the supermarket shelf had the same amount of vitamins.

There are several methods by which an ad can mislead you. One of the most common techniques is called card stacking. In card stacking, the advertiser creates a false impression by omitting important facts. The problem is not in what the ad says but in what it doesn't say. For example, you might see an ad like this:

OUR CANDY BAR COSTS THE SAME TODAY
AS IT DID FIVE YEARS AGO.

The claim made is true. What the ad omits is that the candy bar is now smaller than it was five years ago. Although the price has remained the same, you're getting less for your money today.

Another misleading advertising technique is the interview. This involves an "average person" trying out several brands and selecting the one he or she likes best. Remember, the interview you see on TV is chosen from among hundreds conducted.

A third technique is the use of weasel words. These are words that restrict or limit the promise that an ad appears to be making. For example, a toothpaste ad may state that its product "fights bad breath." The ad is not promising to stop bad breath but only to fight it—a fight it could easily lose. An ad for a skin cream claims that its product "helps cure acne." The terms "help cure" and "cure" are not the same. By using the word "helps," the ad is saying that the product may not do the job by itself.

Advertising can be useful, but it can also be harmful. Look for facts in an ad. Be wary of advertisements that don't say anything specific but try to create images or impressions. Finally, don't buy because of ads alone. See the product, examine it, read the label and warranty, and check the price.

Use advertising; don't let advertising use you.

PLANNING AND SPENDING
A Look at Money Management

Spending money is easy. Spending it wisely is something else again. To get the maximum benefit from your dollars, you must know how to plan and how to shop.

Planning and shopping go hand in hand. You need a plan to tell you what and how much you can buy, and you need sharp shopping skills to get the most value for your money. For example, if your plan includes money for music tapes, you will get more—or better quality—by careful shopping.

Your first step to sound money management is to develop a spending plan to fit your needs, wants, and income. Otherwise, you may find yourself in situations like those described below.

CASE A

POOR PLANNING

Lea received an allowance every Saturday. By Wednesday, she was usually broke. Since her allowance included money to buy lunch at school, Lea had to skip lunch on the last few days of the week.

Jerry's friends were annoyed with him. He was always borrowing money and was slow in paying it back. Jerry received about the same allowance as the others, but it never seemed to be enough for him.

Wendy received a weekly allowance. When it came time for the school trip, she didn't have the money to go. Although she had known about the trip for three months, she never saved up for it.

Lea, Jerry, and Wendy all had one thing in common. They did not know how to budget. A budget is a plan for managing your money that enables you to live within your means. To develop a budget to fit your lifestyle and your wallet, follow these six steps:

1. *Determine your weekly income.* This is the

amount of money you can count on each week. It includes your allowance plus any money that you earn on a regular basis. If you earn money occasionally (shoveling snow, baby-sitting, etc.), don't figure this into your weekly budget. You can put this money into a separate fund to buy something special, but you can't count on it as steady income.

2. *Keep a record of expenses.* Every time you spend money, write it down. At the end of a month, take a look at where your money went. Then ask yourself: If you had it to do over, would you spend your money in the same way?

3. *After seeing where your money went, sort out needs from wants.* Your needs are necessary expenses. They are the things on which you *must* spend money, such as bus fare and school supplies. Your wants are the things you'd like to have but are not necessary. For example, you may *want* to buy records or go to the movies.

4. *Subtract your needs from your income.* The money left is what you can spend on your wants.

5. *Sort your wants into short- and long-range goals.* Short range include such things as going to the movies or buying snacks after school. Long range consists of things for which you must save your money, such as a new bicycle, sports equipment, or a school trip. Always be sure to put some money aside for unexpected situations. You might need to buy a gift for a birthday party, or your bike might break down and require repairs.

6. *Make choices.* This is the most difficult part of budgeting. You can't afford everything you want. If you buy one thing, you'll have to give up something else. Before you buy anything, it's important to think about what you could buy in its place. You may have to make a choice between buying a video tape or going to a concert. Sometimes you may have to choose between immediate pleasure or saving your money to purchase something special.

CASE B

MAKING CHOICES

Janet wanted to buy a portable TV for her room. Her friend Brian wanted to buy one for his room, too. Janet and Brian had just started newspaper routes, and they both received the same pay plus similar tips. Since their income was almost identical, it came as a surprise to their friends when Brian bought his TV three months before Janet purchased hers.

Their friends didn't realize that although Janet and Brian had the same income, they had different expenses. Since Janet came from a large family, she had to put aside a big chunk of money for birthday and holiday gifts. Brian only had to buy presents for his parents and one sister. Janet's home was on the outskirts of town, so she had to pay bus fare to get to school, while Brian lived close enough

---

to walk. Finally, since Janet loved music, she chose to include money in her budget for sheet music, record albums, and concert tickets. Brian's budget included very few luxury expenses. Although their income was the same, their expenses were not.

Janet and Brian had different expenses—both by necessity and choice. Janet had to pay bus fare and Brian didn't. Since Janet's family was larger than Brian's family, it's reasonable that her gift expenses would be more than his. Although Janet could have eliminated money for music items, she chose not to do so. Because music was important to Janet, she made the decision to have the music items now and wait longer for the TV. Brian, on the other hand, cut out all luxuries so he could get the television set as quickly as possible. There is no one "right" way to budget. What's important to you may not be important to someone else. When budgeting, think about all the ways you could spend your money. Then ask yourself the following questions:

• Is what I plan to buy more important to me than what I'll be giving up?

• When I look back on my purchases, will I be satisfied and not regret my decisions?

If the answer to both of the above questions is yes, you know you're using your money in ways that bring you the most satisfaction. If your answer is no, you should sit down and take another look at your spending habits.

CASE C

SETTING GOALS

Michael wanted to buy a bracelet for his mother's birthday. He had seen one in a local jewelry store that he knew she would love. The bracelet was expensive, however, and her birthday was only two months away. Michael knew it would take all of the money he earned mowing lawns for the next eight weeks to afford this special item.

Michael tried hard to save his money, but he couldn't save it all. In order to continue with his lawn business, he needed to buy a part to fix his mower. Then he was asked to contribute to a charity fund-raising drive at school. When the time came to buy the bracelet, Michael did not have the money he needed.

Michael fell victim to a common pitfall of budgeting. He set goals that were too difficult to reach. He should not have planned on buying an item that required him to save all of his earnings. To expect not to spend any money for two months is unrealistic. When determining goals, make sure they are reasonable.

CASE D

HIDDEN EXPENSES

Sara spent most of the money that she had saved from baby-sitting to buy a computer. At the time, it seemed like a fantastic bargain. Unfortunately, to use most of the software designed for it, the computer needed an add-on memory. The software cassettes for this particular brand and model turned out to be more expensive than Sara had realized; and since she didn't have a cassette recorder, she had to buy one. When Sara added up the cost of these items, she realized they came to more than the cost of the computer itself.

Sara's problem was not realizing the hidden costs involved. This situation isn't unique to computers. Hidden expenses can crop up with other types of merchandise, too. For example, if you are interested in photography, your cost doesn't end with the purchase of a camera. You need to buy film and to pay for developing the pictures. Video and electronic games are not only expensive to buy, they are expensive to repair. Suede skirts are beautiful, but the cost of dry cleaning is high. Operating and maintaining products can be costly, and consumers often forget to include these costs when planning their budgets. That's why they're called hidden expenses.

Before buying a product, get a general idea of how much it will cost to use it.

Developing and sticking to a plan is only half the task of sound money management. The other half is shopping wisely. When you shop, you are faced with a wide range of choices. Be sure to get the right product at the best price available.

CASE E

CHECKING OUT THE PRODUCT

Jeremy wanted a bike to ride to school and to deliver newspapers. His best friend, Tony, had just gotten a ten-speed bicycle that was a real beauty. Tony could outrace anyone with his new bike. Jeremy wished he could get one just like it.

Jeremy's parents had promised him a new bike for his birthday, but the ten-speed model cost more than they had planned to spend. Since Jeremy had some money saved, he offered to pay the extra amount. His parents agreed and, on his birthday, they took Jeremy to the store and bought a ten-speed bike.

At first, Jeremy was delighted with the bike. Later on, however, when he went to deliver his newspapers, he ran into difficulty. The bike was hard to balance while carrying the papers. He went back to the store and told the manager about the problem. The manager said

---

> that this was the wrong type of bike to do delivery work.

Jeremy bought the wrong bicycle because he didn't have enough information. Before he made the purchase, he needed to find out about the different types of bicycles. He should have checked what each does well and what each does poorly. If he had taken the time to do this, he would have discovered that a ten-speed bike is great for racing but a poor choice for delivery work. The type of bike known as the "high rise" would have best fit Jeremy's needs.

Finding out about a product before you make a purchase holds for all types of merchandise, not just bicycles. Whether you're buying a home computer, sports equipment, or jewelry, you should follow the four steps listed next:

1. *Decide what you need and want out of the product.* If you're thinking of buying a digital watch, will you be satisfied with one that just tells time, or is it important that it give you the day and date also? If you're shopping for jeans, do you intend to wear them to school, or do you want them for rough-and-tumble sports activities? Once you determine what you want the product to do, you'll be able to decide what features you want the product to have.

2. *Go to the library and read about the product.* Find out all you can about hockey equipment, cameras, hair dryers, or whatever you're thinking of buying. There are magazines that give reports on

product testing. Publications such as *Consumer Reports* can provide you with information on products ranging from VCRs to shampoos. You can find out what brand has the qualities and features that you want. Ask your librarian to help you locate the magazine that you need.

3. *Talk to friends who own the product that you're thinking of buying.* Find out why they bought that particular brand and model. Are they satisfied with it? Ask them about the product's good and bad points.

4. *Examine the product thoroughly.* If it is electronic or mechanical, ask the sales clerk if you can try it out. This way, you can see if it is easy to operate. Be sure to read all labels, warnings, and warranties.

Once you've determined what to buy, your next step is to decide where to buy.

CASE F

SALES GIMMICKS

Elisa had been saving her allowance to buy a new record album. On her way home from school one day, she saw a large sign in the window of Jack's Record Shop that read:

GIGANTIC SALE
BUY ONE ALBUM, GET SECOND ALBUM FREE

Elisa went into the store and bought an album that she liked. Just as promised, the clerk

---

gave her a second album free. Unfortunately, the free album was by an unknown rock group and consisted of songs Elisa had never heard. It certainly wasn't one she would have picked if she had had a choice. Still, since it was free, Elisa thought it was a good deal.

That weekend, she went to her friend Shari's house to listen to records. Shari had just bought an album from Fred's Music Store, and the price tag was still on it. It was the same record that Elisa had bought, but it was only half the price. That meant Shari could buy another album with the savings. Elisa now regretted not shopping at Fred's Music Store. At Jack's Record Shop, she got one album she wanted and one that really didn't interest her. If she had done her shopping at Fred's, she could have gotten two albums of her choice.

Just because something is advertised as a sale, that doesn't mean it's the best price you can get. Beware of so-called bargains that can be purchased elsewhere at less cost. Shop carefully. Some stores have low prices on some merchandise and high prices on other products. Use ads to help you to compare the prices, but be sure you're comparing the same brand and model. Before you buy, make sure the product you want isn't offered somewhere else at a lower price.

CASE G

REFUND POLICY

Jason bought a popular board game to give to his friend Ellen at her birthday party. At the party, he discovered that Ellen already had the game. Jason offered to take his gift back to the store and exchange it for something else. The next day, he tried to return the game, but the manager of the store refused to accept it. She told Jason that the store had a policy of "final sales."

When Jason bought the game, he didn't ask if it could be returned. Before buying anything, find out what the store will do if you want to take the item back. Will you get a refund? Can you exchange it for something else? Do you need a receipt? Is there a time limit on returning merchandise?

Remember, there's more to wise shopping than finding the lowest price. Think twice before buying in a place that has a final-sale policy.

CON GAMES, RACKETS, AND SCHEMES
A Look at Consumer Fraud

Although most business people are honest and law abiding, a small minority prey on the public through the promotion of deceptive practices and con games. Millions of dollars a year are lost by consumers who fall victim to dishonest merchants and unscrupulous swindlers. These operators stretch the law; sometimes, they ignore it completely. Everyone is a potential victim. Since the greatest enemy of the schemer is an informed consumer, it's important to be acquainted with some of the more common schemes and frauds.

CASE A

EARNING SCHEMES

Scott had just started a snow-shoveling service. Although he was making money, the work was hard. He wished he could find an easier way to get the cash to buy all the things he wanted. One weekend, an ad in a magazine caught his attention. It read:

EARN BIG MONEY BY SELLING
HAPPYTIME GREETING CARDS.

Scott read the ad carefully. It seemed easy enough. Each box of cards could be purchased from the Happytime Card Company for two dollars and then sold to friends and neighbors for four dollars. The ad said that you could probably sell up to twenty-five boxes in an hour. Scott thought for a moment. He had earned fifty dollars shoveling snow during the past few weeks. He could take that money and buy twenty-five boxes of cards. If he sold them at four dollars per box, he would have a hundred dollars. It sounded like an easy way to make some quick money. Scott decided to try it.

The next day, he mailed a fifty-dollar money order to the Happytime Card Company. When

---

the cards arrived, he was disappointed. They didn't look much like those pictured in the ad. The cards Scott received were made of cheap-quality paper and had poorly drawn illustrations on the covers. Furthermore, each box contained only four cards. (The ad, of course, had never said how many would be in a box.) Scott wanted to return the merchandise and get his money back. He tried to contact the company, but he found out that they were out of business.

Scott had little success in selling the cards. After more than a month, he had sold only ten boxes—and those mostly to relatives. At four dollars apiece, he had taken in forty dollars. Since it cost him fifty dollars to buy the cards from the company, he ended up losing ten dollars on this so-called money-making venture.

Think twice before entering into a sales plan that requires you to buy the product you'll be selling. Selling is difficult, and the merchandise may not be up to standard. You could find yourself stuck with the product and out the cash. Look for a company that will do the following:

• Allow you to take orders from a catalog or sample pack. This way, you won't be stuck with more merchandise than you can sell.

• Bill you after they've sent the merchandise. This

eliminates sending money to a fly-by-night operation that takes your cash but never sends the product.

• Allow you to return the merchandise if a customer is dissatisfied. This is particularly important if you are selling from a catalog where you don't see the product until after delivery.

How much you earn depends upon the market for the product and the amount of time you are willing to put into selling it. Protect yourself. If you want to get into the sales business, make sure you don't lose money on the deal.

Although the Happytime Card Company didn't break the law, they did mislead Scott into believing that the cards were more attractive than they actually were and that selling would require little time or effort.

CASE B

THE CHAIN LETTER

One day, Anita received a letter in the mail from her friend Sally Hall. It read:

This is a chain letter. It will make you rich if you follow these directions.

Send one dollar to each of the five people listed below. Then, delete the first name and address. Move the four remaining names and addresses up, and add your own as number five. Make five copies of the letter and send to five friends. They, in turn, will send five copies to each of their friends,

---

and the chain will go on endlessly. By the time your name is off the list, you will have received thousands of dollars.

1. Mary Arno
   2222 Beaver Street
   Treetown, Ohio 12345

2. Peter Chin
   123 Chippendale Avenue
   Treetown, Ohio 12345

3. Dave Sandler
   542 Woodland Lane
   Treetown, Ohio 12345

4. Linda Thorpe
   67 Lincoln Avenue
   Lakeview, Ohio 15432

5. Sally Hall
   291 Indian Lake
   Lakeview, Ohio 15432

If you break the chain, you will have bad luck!

Anita didn't know what to think. It seemed easy enough. She decided to continue the chain.

The next day, she mailed a dollar to each of the five people on the list. Then she made five copies of the letter, making sure to delete the first name, move up the other four, and add her name as number five. She mailed the copies to five friends and waited for the dollars to arrive.

When two weeks had passed and Anita had not received any money, she decided to ask her five friends why they had not continued the chain. The first replied that she had received the same letter from two other friends. The second said he was too busy. The third and fourth both said they'd feel embarrassed sending the letter. But it was the response of Anita's fifth friend that was the most surprising. She simply stated that she didn't think the plan would work.

Anita decided to talk to her friend Sally, who had sent her the letter. Sally claimed that she had not fared well either. The only money she received was the dollar from Anita.

Although a chain letter seems simple enough, it just does not work. Chain schemes are mathematically unsound. Someone eventually stops the chain, and the majority of the participants lose their money. If you receive a chain letter asking you to send cash, the best thing you can do is throw the letter out.

CASE C

CHARITY FRAUD

Every year, the students at Jackson High School hold a bazaar to raise money for a charity. This year, Jennifer, the president of the student government, received a letter from an organization called Helpers. Jennifer had never heard of this group, but the letter said their purpose was to raise funds for medical research. The letter went on to ask the student government for a donation. Jennifer and the other school officers thought it was a worthy cause and decided that the money from this year's bazaar would go to Helpers.

The students worked hard on the bazaar. They raised several hundred dollars which they promptly sent to Helpers. About a month later, Jennifer saw a small newspaper article exposing Helpers as a fraud. The money collected was never used for medical research but instead went directly into the pockets of the "directors" of the so-called charity. Jennifer was angry. The students at Jackson High School had sent their money to a phony organization.

Never send money to an unknown charity until you check it out. Instead of helping a worthy cause, your money may be helping someone get rich. Unfortunately, millions of dollars a year are given to phony charities from a generous and unsuspecting public. Before dealing with an organization, make sure it's legitimate. Don't be misled by fancy letters or brochures; they're easy to fake. Check out the charity with the attorney general's office in your state.

CASE D

PHONY CONTESTS

All of Peter's friends were talking about the contest going on at Friendly Ted's Record Shop. When you went to the store, you were given a puzzle to take home and solve. If you came up with the correct solution within a week, you would win a cash prize.

Peter did not usually shop at Friendly Ted's Record Shop, which was known for its high prices. Still, the puzzle contest intrigued him. Since you didn't have to buy anything to enter the contest, Peter decided to give it a try. That afternoon, he went to Friendly Ted's Record Shop and picked up a puzzle and entry form.

He started working on the puzzle that evening. It was so easy that he solved it in less than ten minutes. The next day, Peter went to the store to collect his prize. Instead of money, however, the manager gave him a packet of coupons. Each coupon was worth five dollars toward any purchase made in the store totaling fifteen dollars or more. Peter was disappointed. He had expected a cash prize. As he took a quick look around the store, Peter thought the prices seemed even higher now than they had been in the past. Normally, he would not have purchased a record here, but since he had the coupons, he decided that he should buy something.

Peter didn't win a real prize. The coupons were a slick sales gimmick to get him to buy merchandise. He should have been suspicious when he solved the puzzle so quickly. It was deliberately designed so almost anyone could solve it.

Beware of contests that require you to spend money before you can collect your winnings. If you must buy something or pay a fee before you can get your prize, it's not a bona fide contest. It's just a come-on to get you to make a purchase. The merchandise is usually marked up to make up for the discount. An item that is normally priced at ten dollars may be marked up to twenty dollars, and then a ten-dollar coupon is offered. Your actual saving is zero.

CASE E

COUNTERFEIT BRANDS

When Rachel and her friend Maria were walking through the city, they noticed a crowd gathered at a street corner. A man had set up a table and was selling brand-name jeans for half the usual price. Rachel wanted to buy a good pair of jeans, so Maria suggested that she get them here and buy other things with the money she saved. At first, Rachel hesitated. She always bought her clothes from neighborhood shops or department stores. But Maria convinced her that these jeans were too

---

much of a bargain to turn down. After all, they were a well-known brand, and everyone knows it's the brand that counts, not the store. Finally, Rachel decided to buy from the street vendor.

Later on, when she tried on the jeans at home, she was dissatisfied with the fit. This surprised her because she owned several pairs of this brand and never had had trouble before. After the first wearing, the stitching started to fray. Rachel was annoyed and sent a letter of complaint to the manufacturer.

The manufacturer's representative replied that Rachel had probably purchased counterfeit jeans. These poor-quality jeans, bearing phony labels, were being sold by fly-by-night operators who would set up a street-corner table one afternoon and be gone the next day. The company was upset by the counterfeiting operation and was working with the authorities to apprehend the counterfeiters but could not be responsible for Rachel's purchase. The representative suggested that Rachel be more careful the next time she went shopping.

Counterfeiting brand names can be big business. In one instance, a raid on a New York City warehouse netted thousands of phony brand-name watches as well as watch parts, tools, and counterfeiting equipment. Under this scheme, the brand name on ten-dollar foreign-made watches had been altered to deceive buyers. The brand name Aseikon became Seiko, the Romega brand was counterfeited to read Omega, and the name on Bulovar watches was altered to resemble Bulova.

To avoid being taken by brand-name counterfeiters, make sure you deal with reputable stores. Be wary of street vendors. Even if the merchandise is legitimate, you forfeit your rights to service and adjustments. Where you buy can be as important as what you buy.

CASE F

TRAVEL SCAMS

Mrs. Morgan's history class was planning a trip to Washington, D.C. A student committee had been formed to check out the various tour companies and to select the one that gave the best deal. After looking through assorted brochures, the committee chose Tally Tours. Although none of the students knew anything about this company, their price for the trip was the lowest available.

About one month before the trip, the tour company requested that the students pay in full. The committee collected the money and paid the tour operator the total amount due. Two weeks later, the students received some

---

bad news. The tour operator had disappeared and had taken the money with him. Members of the school committee checked and found that no reservations had been made for the airline or the hotel rooms. Tally Tours was nothing more than a scam. The tour company had offered trip arrangements at low cost, collected the money, and then skipped town with the cash.

There are ways to protect yourself against the type of tour company that swindled Mrs. Morgan's class. First of all, never prepay the total cost of a trip without receiving written confirmation from the hotel and airline. Secondly, make sure you deal with a reliable, established tour operator. Although companies with fine reputations can go bankrupt, they are a better risk than a fly-by-night whose only objective is to take your money and run.

CASE G

MODEL AGENCIES

Teri had always wanted to be a model. One day, she saw an advertisement seeking teenage models. The ad gave a phone number to call to set up an appointment with the T&T Model Agency located in a nearby town.

Teri called, set up an appointment, and went

with her mother on Saturday for an interview. (The agency required a parent present for all prospective clients under eighteen years of age.) The agency representative, Mr. Broom, told Teri that he was sure the agency could get her several modeling assignments. He added that the agency worked on a commission basis and would be paid only if Teri had a modeling job. Since Teri and her mother thought this sounded legitimate, they signed the necessary papers.

As Teri and her mother were leaving the agency, Mr. Broom informed them that Teri would need a photo portfolio and he gave them the name of a photographer to use. Teri said she had some great pictures at home, but Mr. Broom said they wouldn't do. The photos had to be taken by the photographer that T&T recommended. Teri and her mother reluctantly agreed. One year later, they had paid out several hundred dollars for photographs, and Teri still hadn't received a modeling assignment.

Stay away from model or talent agencies that require you to have photographs taken by a specific photographer or voice lessons from a specific school. These agencies are not interested in getting you modeling or acting assignments; they are making their money from the photos or lessons. Either they own the photography studio (or voice school), or they receive a kickback for each customer they supply.

The schemes covered in this chapter are but a few of the many designed to separate you from your money. While some are illegal, others are not. Many are deliberately set up to operate within the law. Once you've lost money through fraud, it's rare that you will ever get it back. It's not enough to know what the schemes are and how they work. It's important to understand the human weaknesses which make us all susceptible.

The swindler relies for success upon universal desires, such as the desires to be healthy, attractive, popular, and rich. The schemer tries to convince you that he can satisfy one or more of these desires. He makes promises he can't keep, takes advantage of your lack of knowledge, and tries to discourage you from investigating further.

Don't become one of the millions of consumers who are taken each year. Make sure you read all documents and get all questions answered before you part with any money. Be wary of any salesperson who discourages questions or tries to pressure you into doing business right away. Before dealing with an unfamiliar company, check it out. Contact your local department of consumer affairs, Better Business Bureau, or your state's attorney general. Finally, and most importantly, be suspicious of "great deals." If something looked like fraud, you wouldn't fall for it. Most schemes and rackets *appear* legitimate. Remember, nothing is free in the marketplace. If something sounds too good to be true, it probably is.

4

WHEN YOU SEND AWAY
A Look at Mail-Order Problems

A comic-book ad for "a six-foot ghost" described the product as having "an inflatable head with a white shroud body" and claimed it could "rise, fall, dart, and dance." The ghost turned out to be a balloon, a six-foot piece of plastic, and a spool of wire.

A magazine ad featuring "an assortment of elegant and fun jewelry" showed a picture of more than twenty-five pieces of attractive costume jewelry. The package mailed out consisted of five plastic items that broke apart within a few weeks.

An ad on a bubble-gum wrapper offered "free information on body building" on receipt of two dollars for postage and handling. The "free information" turned out to be a brochure selling a ten-week course.

The situations described above are all true. When you order through the mail, you buy sight unseen. You don't see the merchandise until after you've paid for it. Unfortunately, what you get is not always what you expect. The following cases involve mail-order problems that you might experience. Luckily, each problem can be prevented if you are aware of the pitfalls to avoid.

CASE A

MAILING MONEY

Beth decided to send away for a bracelet advertised in her favorite magazine. She carefully filled out the order form at the bottom of the ad and placed it in an envelope with some crisp new bills. The next day, she mailed the order to the company.

Four months passed and Beth had not received the bracelet. She told her best friend, Amanda, what had happened. Amanda told Beth to write a letter to the company asking what was causing the delay.

Beth followed Amanda's advice and soon

---

received a reply from the mail-order firm. The company claimed to have no record of receiving her order or her money. Since Beth had mailed cash instead of a check, she couldn't prove that she had sent anything. As a result, Beth never received the bracelet and she never got her money back.

Beth's mistake was mailing cash. When you send cash, the mail-order firm can argue that they never received it, and you can't prove otherwise. If you want to send away for a product, get a money order from a bank or post-office branch so that you'll have a receipt. Better still, ask your parents to write a check. They will eventually get the canceled check back in the mail as their proof of payment. Whatever you do, never send cash.

CASE B

KEEPING RECORDS

Jason was angry. He had sent away for five music tapes, but the package contained only three. Jason wanted to write a letter to the firm telling them about the missing tapes, but he had thrown out the magazine that ran the ad for the tapes and he didn't remember the address of the company.

Forgetting to jot down the location of a mail-order firm is a common mistake. When sending away for merchandise, be sure to keep a record of your order, especially the company's address. Two frequent mail-order problems involve never receiving the merchandise or, as in the above case, receiving an incorrect order. These situations often are caused by simple clerical errors and can be straightened out by writing to the firm. If you don't know the company's address, you can't write.

If possible, keep the original ad or a copy of the ad as part of your record. If the product you receive differs from the ad's description, you can ask a consumer-affairs agency to help you get your money back; but they may require the ad as proof. Be sure to keep the ad where you can find it when you need it.

CASE C

VAGUE DESCRIPTIONS

While browsing through a catalog, Maria saw an ad for a model of a jet plane. It read:

LARGE MODEL OF JET PLANE
MAKES AN IDEAL GIFT

The ad included a photo of the model on top of a bookcase. Maria thought the plane would be a perfect gift for her brother's birthday, so she decided to send away for it.

A week before the birthday, Maria received a small package in the mail. She could not imagine what was in it. The package was too small to contain the model plane. As she opened the box, a look of disappointment spread across her face. It *was* the plane. It was made of plastic and was only five inches long.

Maria quickly ran into her room and looked up the ad in the catalog. As she reread it, she noted that the size of the model was never mentioned. Maria had just assumed that the plane would be at least a foot in length. Now, looking carefully at the ad, she noticed some small print at the bottom of the page. It said that the plane in the photo was just one in an assortment of many models and that the firm reserved the right to send whichever model they wished.

It's important to search an ad carefully for a precise description. Look for the exact measurements of the product as well as the type of material used to make it. (Products that appear to be made of wood often turn out to be made of plastic.) Beware of general terms such as "beautiful" or "colossal." These terms create an image but tell you nothing about the merchandise.

Pictures can be deceiving, too. If a company

intends to send a product that differs from the photograph used, the ad should tell you so. Unfortunately, this may not be the first thing to catch your eye. You must read everything in an ad, including the small print. A recent ad in a comic book headlined free iron-on transfers while the small print demanded $2.50 for postage and handling. Another ad, this one in a teen magazine, pictured an assortment of more than thirty cosmetics. At the bottom of the ad in small print was this: "You will receive at least five of the items shown above."

Those who looked only at the photo assumed they would get more than two dozen cosmetics. Legally, the company was required to send no more than five items. That was the minimum promised in the small print. You won't go wrong if you remember the consumer proverb: "What the large print giveth, the small print taketh away."

CASE D

DELIVERY TIME

Joe was looking forward to going camping with his friends during summer vacation. One night, about three weeks before his trip, he saw an ad in a magazine for a knapsack. Joe needed a knapsack for his trip, and this one was exactly the type he wanted. Since the ad promised to rush delivery in less than ten days, Joe assumed it would arrive in plenty of time.

> The weeks passed by quickly, and the item never came. The day before his camping trip, Joe thought about going to a local store and buying a knapsack. Although he had enough money saved to do this, he'd then be stuck with two knapsacks when the mail-order package finally arrived. Joe didn't know what to do.

Joe wasn't aware of it, but there was an easy solution to his problem. The mail-order company was in violation of federal law. According to law, a company that promises to send merchandise by a specific time must do so. If no time is included in the ad, the merchandise must be shipped to you within thirty days. In either case, if there is a delay, the company must notify you of the new delivery date and inform you of your right to accept this new date or to cancel for a full refund. The refund must be sent to you within seven days.

Although legitimate mail-order firms abide by this ruling, some "less than reputable" companies may not send you a notice, hoping you're not aware of your rights. Since no one wants to order a present for Aunt Sophie and have it arrive five weeks after her birthday, or send for a ski hat that finally comes in July, it's important for you to take action. If you don't receive a notice on a delayed delivery and you want to cancel, write a letter to the company informing them of your decision. Let them know that if you don't receive your refund, you will contact your local consumer affairs agency or the postal inspector in your area. (Before writing this letter, check your dates to make sure the delivery is past due.)

Exempt from this law covering delayed deliveries are mail-order plants and seeds, photo developing and processing, C.O.D. orders, and magazine subscriptions (except the first issue).

CASE E

UNORDERED MERCHANDISE

One afternoon, when Jan arrived home from school, there was a package waiting for her. She opened it and took out a leather packet filled with coins from different countries. She was wondering who had sent them to her, when she noticed a letter at the bottom of the box. According to the letter, the coins had been sent to her "on approval" for one week. During the next seven days, she was to look over the packet and decide whether or not she wanted it. If she chose to keep the coins, she was to mail a check to the company for the amount specified in the letter. If she didn't want the merchandise, she was to return it. Jan was both puzzled and annoyed. She had not ordered anything on approval. Although she liked the coin collection, she didn't think it was worth the price. On the other hand, why

---

should she be required to pay the postage to return something she never ordered in the first place?

Jan was *not* required to return the coin collection. Unfortunately, she wasn't aware that the law says you don't have to pay for unordered merchandise. In fact, only two types of merchandise can legally be sent to you without your consent:
  • free samples which are clearly marked.
  • merchandise mailed by a charity asking for a donation. (You don't have to give, and you don't have to return the merchandise.)
In all other instances, it is illegal for a firm to send merchandise to you unless you request it.

CASE F

TOO GOOD TO BE TRUE

As Nancy was reading her favorite magazine, a small ad at the bottom of the page caught her eye. It read:

GET RID OF ACNE WITH NEW TOBO CREAM
CLEANS UP SKIN IN TEN DAYS

Nancy had terrible skin problems. She was going to a doctor for treatment, but the doctor told her it would be months before she'd see any results. Tobo seemed to be the answer to

Nancy's problem. As she checked the ad, she discovered that the cream was not available in stores. It had to be purchased directly from the ZeeBee Pharmaceutical Company. Nancy had never heard of this company, but she decided to send for the product anyway.

Three months passed and Nancy still had not received any Tobo cream. One day, as she was reading a newspaper, an article on one of the back pages caught her eye. It was about two men who had just been arrested. This pair had formed a company named ZeeBee Pharmaceutical and advertised a fake remedy for acne called Tobo cream. After cashing all the checks and money orders that people sent, the men left town. By the time the police caught up with them, it was too late. All the money had been spent. There was nothing left to return to the hundreds of people who had ordered and paid for this phony product.

There are no magical potions guaranteed to get rid of acne instantly, take off fat, or make you grow. Be suspicious of any ad that promises a miraculous cure. It probably is a scheme to take your money and not give you anything in return.

It can also be a mistake to deal with an unfamiliar company. Do business with reliable firms. If you've never heard of a company, check it out before you order any merchandise. Write to the Better Business Bureau or the department of consumer affairs in the city or county where the company is located. Ask if they have a record of complaints about that business.

CASE G

CUSTOMER ERRORS

When the package arrived in the mail from the ABX Mail Order House, Frank assumed it was the new poster that he had ordered for his room. When he opened the box, he found a pair of women's slippers. Frank had heard about companies mixing up orders, but this was the first time it had happened to him. The next day, Frank sat down and wrote to ABX, informing them that they had sent the wrong item. He then mailed the package back to them, along with his letter.

Several weeks later, Frank received a note from ABX. It turned out that Frank, not the mail-order house, had made the mistake. When he ordered the poster, he copied down the wrong code number on the order form. Instead of checking off box #301, which was the number for the poster, he had checked the box directly underneath it, #302. Luckily for Frank, the company wanted satisfied customers. They wrote that they would send the poster

---

> anyway. Although Frank did eventually receive the right item, his mistake delayed delivery.

Not all errors are company caused. Customers can make mistakes, too. Check your order for accuracy. If you must copy a code number onto a form, copy it correctly. If you are required to check off a box, check the right one. Include size, color, and other information needed to complete the purchase. Finally, write neatly, so the clerks at the mail-order house can read your order or so the computers don't reject the information.

Even if you follow the advice given in this chapter, you still could face problems. Unfortunately, some firms don't deliver what their ads promise. If this happens to you, write to the mail-order house and to the editor of the publication that carried the ad. If you don't get results, contact your local consumer affairs agency. If you don't have a local agency, go to the nearest post-office branch and ask to be put in touch with the postal inspector for your area. If fraud was involved, he or she can investigate and take action against the company.

Receiving mail-order merchandise can be fun, but there also can be problems. You can go a long way in protecting yourself if you know the pitfalls to avoid.

IT'S IN THE SMALL PRINT
A Look at Labels and Warranties

The best consumer advice is summed up in one word—READ. Information to help you make smart purchasing decisions is available on labels and warranties. This information won't do you any good, however, unless you read it. Failure to do this can result in costly mistakes. If you just take a few minutes and read the printed material that can be found on or near the merchandise for sale, you will avoid some common pitfalls of buying.

CASE A

THE SIZE GAME

Jessica's two best friends were going to be staying overnight for a pajama party. A few hours before the girls arrived, Jessica went to the store to buy some potato chips. At first, she planned to buy a regular-size bag; but then she noticed the Jumbo Party Pack. This bag cost only a little more than the regular-size package but it looked twice as large. Jessica decided to buy the Jumbo Party Pack.

When Jessica arrived home, she emptied the bag into a large bowl. To her surprise, the chips filled only about one-third of the dish. She looked at the weight listed on the package and discovered that it was eight ounces. Then she remembered that the regular-size bag was eight ounces, too. Although the Jumbo Party Pack looked twice as large as the regular bag, they held the same amount.

Don't be fooled by the size of the packaging. A big box may actually hold less than a smaller one. Watch out for terms such as "Family Size" or "Large Economy Size." They don't tell you how much of the product you'll really be getting. Instead, check weights and prices and then figure which item gives you the most for your money.

Sometimes, determining the cost per ounce is difficult. Weights are often given in fractions such as "22½ ounces." Some stores will provide shelf signs with information on the cost per ounce or per pound. This is called unit pricing. If the stores in your community don't use unit pricing, you'll have to do the math yourself. Whatever you do, however, don't buy just because of the package's appearance. You mislead yourself by assuming that because one package is larger than another, it contains more of the product.

CASE B

CARE LABELS

Mary bought a beautiful blue sweater with the money she received for her birthday. The first time she wore it was to a friend's party, where she spilled juice on it. When Mary arrived home from the party, she changed her outfit and put all the clothes she had been wearing into the washing machine. After the laundry was done, she checked the sweater carefully. The stain was gone.

One week later, when Mary put the sweater on, she discovered that it had shrunk. She took the sweater back to the store where she had bought it. When she told the manager what had happened, he replied that certain types of clothing should not be machine washed and dried. He then showed her the label on the inside of the sweater that read "Dry Clean Only." If Mary had read this earlier, she would have known that she should not wash the sweater.

Read the care label when you buy clothing. The law says that clothing costing more than three dollars must have a permanent label attached that gives instruction for care. (This law does not apply to footwear, headwear, or gloves.) By reading the label, you will find out how to wash, dry, iron, bleach, or otherwise care for a particular article of clothing. If you check the label before you buy, you can determine how costly it will be to care for an item. (Dry cleaning, for example, is expensive.) Finally, following care instructions will prevent you from making mistakes such as using a hot iron when a cool one is needed, bleaching material that should not be bleached, or washing clothing that should be dry cleaned.

CASE C

WHAT'S NOT INCLUDED

When Dave went to the store, he bought a battery-operated calculator on sale. As soon as he got home, he took the item out of the box. To his surprise, it didn't work. Only then did Dave notice the writing on the side of the package that said:

NEEDS 4 C BATTERIES

BATTERIES NOT INCLUDED

The product would not work without batteries, and Dave didn't have any money left to buy them. He would have to save up to buy the batteries, so it would be a few weeks before he'd be using his new calculator.

It's no fun to buy something that won't work when you get it home. Before making a purchase, read the label on the box carefully. Be sure you know the answers to the following:

• Do you need to buy anything extra to make the item work?

• Does the product come unassembled? (This means *you* have to put it together.)

• Are there any warnings for the safe use of the item?

The information on the package can help you to use and to enjoy the product you buy. Before making a purchase, be sure you read this information.

Reading the label on a box will give you valuable facts about the product inside. Equally important, however, is to check out an item's warranty before you make your final decision to buy.

A warranty is a guarantee. It's the manufacturer's

promise to stand behind its merchandise. All merchandise is covered by what is known as an "implied warranty." This means the product is expected to perform the function for which it is sold. For example, a hair dryer must dry hair. The only way a seller can get out of an implied warranty is by stating in writing that there is no warranty at all: "As is." Otherwise, you get the implied warranty as well as any written warranty given by the manufacturer. (Some states do not permit "as is" sales.)

Written warranties come with most major purchases, although this is not legally required. A written warranty spells out what the manufacturer will do if there is something wrong with the product you buy. Will the manufacturer fix it? For how long? Are all parts and labor costs covered? If the product can't be fixed, will it be replaced?

The law enables you to check out a warranty before making a purchase. Any warranty given on merchandise costing more than fifteen dollars must be available for you to look at in the store. All warranties must be easy to read and understand. They must be written in ordinary language, not "legalese."

Knowing that products do break down, you should read your warranties carefully so that if you experience a problem, you'll know exactly what to do.

CASE D

PROOF OF PURCHASE

Gordon's radio broke down a few weeks after he had bought it. Since the warranty was for six months, he simply took the broken item to the manufacturer's service center to be repaired. The manager of the center said she would be glad to fix the radio as long as Gordon had a dated sales slip to show that he had bought the product during the past six months. The sales receipt was needed as proof that the merchandise was still covered under the warranty period. The manager added that this requirement was spelled out in the warranty. Unfortunately, Gordon hadn't read the warranty carefully when he purchased the radio. He never realized that he needed to save the sales slip. Now it was too late. He had thrown out the sales receipt long ago.

Since most warranties only cover a specific length of time after purchase, you will usually have to prove when you bought the product. Your warranty will spell out how to do this. Some companies may require you to register your purchase by filling out and submitting a card when you buy the product. Most of the time, however, a dated sales slip is proof enough. Be sure to keep your sales receipt with your warranty so that if the product breaks down, your proof of purchase date is readily available.

CASE E

FULL vs. LIMITED

The small television set that Angela had purchased with her newspaper-route earnings was a real bargain—or so she thought. Two months later, however, the sound failed and Angela discovered that the warranty did not cover the total cost of repair. Angela thought she had a full warranty on the TV. A full warranty means the manufacturer will fix the item free of charge. What Angela had, however, was a full warranty on the picture tube only. The rest of the set, including the sound system, was covered by a limited warranty. Under a limited warranty, the manufacturer can charge you for a portion of the repair costs.

If you see the word "full," don't stop reading and assume that everything is covered. A product can have more than one written warranty. It can have a full warranty on part of the item and a limited warranty on the rest. Before buying a product, read the warranty carefully and find out exactly what is covered.

CASE F

GETTING SERVICE

Joey thought that his new stereo had a good warranty, although he hadn't read it. The sales clerk had said that all parts and labor costs were covered for one year. During that period, when one of the speakers broke, Joey checked the warranty to find out where to take the broken item to be repaired. As he read the warranty, he came across the following:

MAIL THE STEREO SYSTEM, POSTAGE PAID,
TO ONE OF THE SERVICE CENTERS
LISTED BELOW.

Joey looked at the list of locations of the repair centers. The closest one to him was in another state. "Postage paid" meant that Joey would have to pay for the mailing. The stereo system was no small item to mail. Although the manufacturer fixed the broken item free of charge as promised under the warranty, getting the product to the repair center took a large chunk out of Joey's wallet.

As Joey found out, mailing merchandise to a service center is not cheap. Think of all the products for which warranties are given: stereos, hair blowers, bicycles, VCRs, computers, electronic toys. None of these items will fit into a normal-size envelope. They are all costly to mail. Be aware that there are manufacturers who will require you to pay this expense. On the other hand, some companies will pay the mailing cost, or they will simply require you to take the merchandise back to the store where you bought it. Whatever the manufacturer's policy, it will be written in the warranty. Before purchasing a product, check what you'll have to do to get service if and when you need it.

In the three preceding cases, Gordon, Angela, and Joey all had different problems stemming from the same root: They didn't read the warranty until it was too late. Make sure you read the warranty prior to making a purchase and that you check for the following:

• Does it cover the entire product or only certain parts? (If some parts are not covered, find out how likely they are to break and how expensive they are to repair.)

• Are labor costs covered or only replacement of parts?

• How long does the warranty last? Are all parts covered for the same length of time?

• What do you have to do to get service? Are you required to ship a heavy product to the factory?

• Is there anything you must do, such as send in a warranty card or deal only with an authorized service center, to keep the warranty valid?

• What will the company do if the product fails repeatedly?

Remember, a warranty can offer valuable service and protection, but it also can rob you of your rights. What is not covered is often more significant than what is covered. To avoid problems later on, read the warranty and make sure you understand all of its provisions before you make your purchase.

6

KEEP IT SAFE
A Look at Product Safety

Every year, thirty-three million people are injured in product-related accidents. Some are disabled for life while others don't even make it out of the hospital. Whether you're buying a gift for a younger brother or sister, baby-sitting for a neighbor's child, or using your own sports equipment, knowing how to recognize and avoid potential hazards is important. Although no one can eliminate all the dangers, everyone can observe safety precautions in buying, using, and maintaining products.

CASE A

THE BABY TOY

When Joyce's brother was born, she bought a mobile to hang in his room. The mobile had three little yellow ducks dangling from a long string. On the day her mother and new brother came home from the hospital, Joyce hung the mobile over the crib. Later on, when Joyce looked in the room, she noticed that the mobile was no longer there. When she asked her parents about this, her mother replied that she had taken the mobile away because its string was too long to be hanging over the baby's bed. If it fell into the crib, the baby could strangle on it. Joyce was horrified. How could something as pretty and innocent looking as three little ducks on a string be so deadly?

When buying for an infant or toddler, remember that cute and cuddly doesn't also mean safe. A soft teddy bear may have button eyes that can come off and be swallowed. A hand-painted doll may be made with toxic material. To select a safe gift for a baby or young child, do the following:

• Look for toys that are too large for a child to swallow.

• Make sure there are no small, detachable parts that can become lodged in ears, nose, or throat.

• Avoid products that have sharp points or edges.

Also stay away from items made of glass or brittle plastic that could break into small, jagged pieces.

• Look for the word "nontoxic" on the box or label. (This is especially important because babies frequently put toys in their mouths.) Check the label on fabric products for a "nonflammable" fire-resistant notice.

• Make sure the toy doesn't have a long string or chain that can be wrapped around a child's neck.

The U.S. government, through its Product Safety Commission, strives to keep dangerous toys off the market. Still, some manage to be sold in this country every year. Remember, there is no substitute for your own thorough and careful examination of a toy before you buy it.

CASE B

THE AGE FACTOR

John's younger sister, Allison, loved arts and crafts. She enjoyed working with crayons, finger paints, and clay. When John went shopping to buy a gift for his sister's sixth birthday, he spotted a jewelry-making set that he decided would be perfect for her. It came with a small oven for baking the jewelry. Although the label stated "Not Recommended for Children Under 8 Years of Age," he bought it anyway. His sister was creative, and he thought that the jewelry kit would not be too difficult for her.

Allison loved her brother's gift. Then one Saturday, while she was working with the kit, she accidentally touched the oven's heating element and burned her hand.

By law, no item with a heating element may be recommended for children under eight years of age. Just because a child is creative or good with crafts, it doesn't mean he or she is mature enough to operate such an item safely. Some toys, such as chemistry sets or craft kits, are fine for older children but dangerous for younger children. Before buying a gift for a younger brother or sister, look for an age recommendation on the box.

CASE C

BROKEN PRODUCTS

It was raining, and Timothy and Brian were bored. They decided to go down to the basement. There was an old trunk down there, and the boys thought they might find something to amuse themselves. As Timothy looked through the trunk, he came across an old broken dart set. There was only one dart left, and the rubber tip had come off the end of it. Now it ended with a sharp point. Timothy knew his parents were busy upstairs and wouldn't be able to fix the dart until later in the day. Since Timothy didn't want

> to wait, he decided to play with the dart set in its present condition.
>
> Timothy put the dart board up on the far side of the basement. Brian stood a few feet away. Timothy went first. Unfortunately, he was not a good shot. He missed the board but he didn't miss his friend. The dart hit Brian on the arm.

Never play with a broken product. Without rubber tips, the darts were too dangerous to use. Brian was lucky that the dart hit him on the arm and not in the eye.

Often, products that are fine to use in good condition can be hazardous when broken. For example, a bike with a loose wheel can cause accidents, or an electrically operated game with a frayed wire can give the user a shock. Be sure you read any safety rules that come with a product and that you follow the manufacturer's instructions for proper maintenance. Finally, before using an item, check to see that all its parts are intact and operating correctly.

> ### CASE D
>
> ### SAFETY EQUIPMENT
>
> Fred enjoyed roller skating and he was good at it. He was a careful skater, too. His skates fit him well, and he kept them in good condition. He also checked his skating surface be-

fore and while skating. He looked for broken cement and branches or gravel in his path. Despite his safety precautions, while Fred was skating to a friend's house one day, he fell down and broke his elbow.

Although Fred followed safety precautions, he forgot an important one. He needed to wear elbow pads. Even a good skater can have an accident. You can't always avoid falling, but you might prevent broken bones if you wear protective safety equipment such as elbow and knee pads. Whenever you participate in a sport or engage in any physical activity, there is a chance of injury. You can minimize this chance, however, if you know and follow all the safety rules.

CASE E

BIKE SAFETY

Megan's new bike had all sorts of special features. Megan especially liked the hand brakes. They required less effort to use than the foot brakes on her old bike and they were more fun to operate, too.

The first time Megan rode her new bike was to school. On the way, it started to rain; but that didn't worry Megan. She had ridden in the rain many times before.

Megan saw the traffic light at the end of the block turn red, but she didn't think she'd have to begin stopping until she was much closer to it. As she neared the corner, she applied the brakes. To her dismay, the bike did not come to a halt. Instead, she plowed right into a car that was stopped in front of her.

Megan didn't know the basic safety rules of bike riding. She was not aware that under wet conditions hand brakes do not stop the bike as quickly as they do under dry conditions. If she had started braking earlier, she could have avoided the accident.

In past years, bicycles have had the dubious distinction of ranking at the top of the list of consumer products most frequently associated with severe injuries. Hazards increase for bike riders during the rain and at night. If possible, avoid riding at such times. If you must ride, however, make sure you follow safety precautions. During wet weather, watch your speed and give yourself more time to brake. After dark, wear reflective trim applied to your clothing and be sure your bike reflectors work.

Bike riding is fun, and it can provide a convenient and inexpensive form of transportation. If you keep your bicycle in good shape, obey traffic laws, and use extra caution under hazardous conditions, you'll decrease your chances of accidents and injuries.

CASE F

FOOD POISONING

Since Ginny's mother worked, Ginny usually got dinner ready for the family. She had been helping her mom in the kitchen for several years, so this was not a difficult chore. Today, her mother left a note instructing Ginny to prepare hamburgers, mashed potatoes, and green beans. As Ginny took the can of green beans out of the cabinet, she noticed that the ends were bulging. Ginny had never seen a can like this. Just to be on the safe side, she decided to cook another vegetable for dinner.

Ginny did the right thing. The can of green beans could have been infected with the deadly bacteria that cause botulism. Botulism causes progressive respiratory paralysis with a fatality rate of about 65 percent in the United States.

Damage to the outside of the can doesn't always mean that bacteria are present. Rusts or dents don't affect the contents, providing the can doesn't leak. Bulging ends, leaks, or food that has an abnormal odor or appearance, however, can be a sign of bacteria. If you have a can that exhibits any of those characteristics, throw it out *without tasting the food.*

CASE G

GIVING MEDICINE

Jean had just gotten her first baby-sitting job. She was going to watch five-year-old Joshua Lane while his parents went shopping for a new washing machine. When Jean arrived at the Lanes' home, Joshua was eating his lunch. Mrs. Lane told Jean to give her son a vitamin pill when he finished his meal. She said that the children's vitamins were in the top drawer of the kitchen cabinet.

Later on, when Jean checked the cabinet, she found one bottle of pills in the drawer. They looked like vitamins, but there was no label on the container. Jean decided not to give them to Joshua. Although she was pretty sure they were the vitamins, she couldn't be positive. Jean thought it would be better for the boy to wait a few hours until his parents came home than possibly to give him the wrong pill.

Jean did the right thing. Toys and sports equipment are not the only products that can cause injury. Medicines can be harmful or fatal if used incorrectly. If called upon to give or take medicine, follow these rules:

• Never take medicine from an unlabeled bottle. You can prevent labels from falling off bottles by putting transparent tape over them.

• Read the directions and warnings on the label each time you use the product.

• Check the expiration date on all medicines. This is the last date that the medicine should be used. Ask your parents to weed out leftover prescriptions from the medicine cabinet.

• When measuring medicine, pay close attention to what you're doing. Don't take or give medicine in the dark.

In the event of accidental poisoning or an overdose of medicine, immediately call your hospital emergency or poison-control center. Write down their phone numbers and keep them near the telephone.

7

WHAT ARE WE EATING
A Look at Our Foods
and Our Diets

What do you know about the foods you eat? Take the quiz below and see how you score.

TRUE OR FALSE

1. There's more sodium (salt) in one serving (one-half cup) of instant chocolate pudding than in a one-ounce bag of potato chips.

2. A quarter-pound hamburger has more calories than a medium-size baked potato.

3. One ounce of Quaker 100% Natural Cereal has more sugar than one ounce of Cheerios.

4. A product labeled "contains no preservatives" may contain other artificial additives.

5. Decreasing your calorie intake can affect your skin and your hair.

The answers to the five questions are the same—true. If this surprises you, it's no wonder. Myths exist as to what is in the products we eat. Myths are created by mass media that promote a culture of pizza, fried chicken, and candy bars and at the same time bombard the viewer with bone-thin figures in tight designer jeans and bikinis. "Health" foods, "natural" foods, and "diet" foods are all terms tossed around without much thought as to what they actually mean. It can be confusing. Luckily, the facts are available about today's food products. It's important to be aware of these facts, since your diet can affect your looks, personality, academic achievement, and health.

CASE A

EMPTY CALORIES

This was Gordon's first semester in a new school, and his report card was not good. He had always been a B student, but this time all he got were C's and D's. Gordon just couldn't concentrate in class anymore, and he was al-

---

ways nervous and tired. His mother had trouble waking him up in the morning. He got up now at the last minute and only had time to grab a doughnut before he left for school.

Although his grades weren't good, Gordon did like the new school. What he liked best was going out during the lunch period. In his old school, he had brought his lunch from home. Since the new school was next to a fast-food chain, Gordon would go there and have a frankfurter, french fries, and a cola drink every day.

The one thing Gordon didn't like about the new school was the homework he had to do each afternoon. He always made sure he had a big platter of cookies and a bottle of soda to get him through. Unfortunately, when dinnertime came, he was too full to eat. He didn't get hungry until later in the evening, when he'd munch on some chips or candy.

All in all, Gordon liked the new school, but he worried about his grades. He just didn't understand why he couldn't concentrate in class and why he never had any energy.

Gordon's energy and concentration problems probably stemmed from his diet—a diet of empty calories. He filled up on foods that were high in fats and carbohydrates but low in the essential nutrients that he needed.

Your body requires protein, vitamins, and minerals to stay healthy and grow. A diet lacking these nutrients can lead to fatigue, irritability, hair loss, skin dryness, muscle cramps, and more serious medical disorders including dehydration and hypokalemia (a potassium imbalance that can cause death).

To make sure that your body gets the nutrients it needs, you should eat foods from the following four basic food groups each day:

1. *Milk group* (milk, cheese, yogurt, ice cream). Four servings daily. Count an eight-ounce glass of milk, an ounce of cheese, eight ounces of yogurt, or one and one-half cups of ice cream as a serving.

2. *Fruit and vegetable group* (especially dark leafy-green vegetables and yellow vegetables such as carrots and squash). Four or more servings each day.

3. *Bread and cereal group* (whole grain and enriched bread, cereal, and macaroni and rice products). Four or more servings daily. Count one slice of bread, one cup of dry cereal, or one-half cup of macaroni or rice as a serving.

4. *Meat group* (meat, poultry, fish, eggs, dry beans, and nuts). Two servings daily. Count three ounces of meat, poultry, or fish, two eggs, or four tablespoons of peanut butter as a serving.

An occasional doughnut, candy bar, or soda is okay. Just remember, they provide little in the way of nutrients. You can get along without these foods and be perfectly healthy. They are luxuries. Get the necessities first.

CASE B

FAD DIETS

Stacy was constantly on a diet. It seemed she was always on a different type of diet, too. There was the yogurt diet, the grapefruit diet, the protein diet, and so on. Whenever Stacy heard about a new fad diet, she tried it.

Although Stacy lost weight on these diets, she always gained it back quickly. The last time she had dieted, she had dropped ten pounds in two weeks but gained it all back in three more weeks. She was beginning to get discouraged. She wondered if there was any way she could lose weight and keep it off.

Crash diets usually result in a fast but *temporary* weight loss. Pounds lost quickly are gained back quickly. If you lose weight gradually, you'll have better luck keeping it off.

Fad diets not only have short-term weight-loss effects but can also severely damage your health. A fad diet is usually not a balanced diet and it may not provide you with sufficient nutrition. It may lack foods that are high in a specific vitamin or mineral that you need. A balanced diet is especially important while your body is still developing. Before going on any weight-reduction program, check with your doctor. Make sure the diet includes all the vitamins, minerals, and protein that you need for a healthy growing body.

CASE C

THE ATHLETE'S DIET

Luke was thrilled when he made the school football team. He wanted to keep his body in top shape. To do this, he worked out each day, got plenty of sleep, and ate well-balanced meals. Then a friend told him that athletes need more red meat than other people. Luke's family usually had red meat once a week for dinner and ate chicken, fish, and eggs on the other nights. Luke wondered if he should be eating more red meat.

The idea that athletes need more red meat than other people simply isn't true. Since physical activity burns up calories, an athlete may have to eat more food than the nonactive person, but the calories don't have to come from a specific food. Protein is essential, but it can come from fish, poultry, or eggs. The most important thing was for Luke to eat a well-balanced diet that included foods high in protein, as well as fruits, vegetables, whole-grain breads, and cereals. All these nutrients are needed to keep in top condition.

CASE D

DIET FOODS

Jill wanted to lose weight. When she went to the supermarket on Friday, she headed right to the diet section and selected a box of "reduced calorie" brownie mix. She thought this would be the perfect diet snack. She planned to bake the brownies that evening so that whenever she became hungry during the weekend, she'd have something to eat.

The mix made twelve brownies. By the end of the weekend, Jill had eaten them all. The next day, she went to the store to buy more brownie mix. As she picked up the package, she noticed the nutritional information listed on the side of the box. Each brownie had 45 calories. That meant her "diet" snack had totaled 540 calories.

"Reduced calories" doesn't mean that the product has only a few calories. It means that its caloric content must be at least one-third lower than a similar food in which the calories aren't reduced. Thus, even diet foods have to be eaten in moderation.

Foods that are labeled "reduced calories" are required to have listed on the label the number of calories contained in each serving and the size of an average serving. By checking this information, you can be sure of the number of calories you are eating and plan your diet accordingly.

CASE E

"HEALTHY" FOODS

Tom was careful about the foods he ate. His meals were well balanced, and even his snacks were nutritious—or so he thought. When Tom stopped at a store after school, he always bought a granola bar. One day, while he was unwrapping his snack, he happened to glance at the nutrition information on the label. He was amazed at what he saw. This is how the label read:

GRANOLA BAR

Percentage of U.S.
Recommended Daily
Allowances (U.S. RDA)

Protein	2
Vitamin A	*
Vitamin C	*
Thiamin	4
Riboflavin	2
Niacin	*
Calcium	2
Iron	2

*Contains less than 2%
of the U.S. RDA of these nutrients

The granola bar was not particularly high in nutrients. Although granola provides a certain amount of fiber, which is necessary for roughage, this snack still wasn't the "healthy" food that Tom thought it was.

Don't be misled by images or impressions. Go straight for the facts. According to federal law, any food that makes a nutritional or dietary claim must provide the following information on the label:

- A suggested serving size
- The number of servings per container
- Calorie content per serving
- Grams of protein, carbohydrates, fats, and sodium per serving
- Percentage per serving of U.S. Recommended Daily Allowances (RDA) for protein, vitamin A, vitamin C, thiamin, niacin, riboflavin, calcium, and iron. (The U.S. RDA are the amounts of protein, vitamins, and minerals that you should eat each day to keep healthy.)

The law also requires that most food products state their ingredients on the label and that these ingredients be listed in descending order of weight. (This means the ingredient present in the largest amount is the first ingredient listed, and so on down the line.) By checking the ingredients on a package, you can find out what's in that food. Sometimes, you may be surprised at what you find, such as in the following case:

CASE F

THE HIDDEN SUGARS

Mark had acne. His doctor told him that the first step to curing it was to cut out sweets. Since Mark was anxious to clear up his skin problem, he agreed to go on a diet low in sugar. These were the meals he decided to eat on the first day.

BREAKFAST: Fruit & Fibre Cereal
LUNCH: strawberry yogurt
DINNER: hamburger with catsup, baked beans, and green salad with French dressing

Mark thought that meals such as these should do the trick. If he had checked the ingredients in these foods, he would have been surprised. His diet was full of hidden sugar.

One reason to check the ingredient listing is that you might find something you don't expect. For example, although almost everyone knows there's sugar in candy and ice cream, many people are unaware of the large amounts of sugar that can be found in foods such as fruit yogurt and catsup. Here's a breakdown on the sugar content in the foods on Mark's diet. (Since ingredients vary from brand to brand, the ingredient listings with the asterisks are taken from popular national brands.)

Fruit & Fibre. Sugar is the third ingredient listed. Although fruits are nutritious, they do have natural sugar.

* *Strawberry yogurt.* Sugar is the second ingredient listed. (This is because the strawberry flavor comes from fruit preserves, which are full of sugar.)

* *Catsup.* The third ingredient listed on the catsup bottle is corn sweeteners. This is another form of sugar.

* *Baked beans.* Sugar is the fourth ingredient listed.

* *French dressing.* The third ingredient listed is sugar.

Even when you eat a food, you can't always tell what is in it. Catsup isn't sweet-tasting, yet it contains a large amount of sugar. Chocolate pudding doesn't taste salty, but it contains sodium. The only way you can be sure to get what you want is by reading the label. The law requires the food industry to give specific information on the package, but it is up to you to read the label and use this information wisely.

RIGHTING A WRONG
A Look at Effective Complaining

You buy a loaf of bread to make sandwiches for the class picnic. On opening the package, you discover that it's moldy. You throw it out and go to the store to buy another loaf.

The watch you received for your birthday, two months ago, doesn't keep the right time. You take it to the repair center twice, but they don't fix it properly. You stick this new watch in a drawer and wear an old one.

You go to a fast-food chain for lunch and order a cola with your meal. The waitress brings you a root beer instead. You really wanted the cola, but you drink the root beer anyway.

If you have a valid complaint, it's important that you bring it to the attention of the right person. But it's not enough just to complain. To increase the chances of getting your problem resolved, you must complain effectively. This chapter will look at the basic rules of the art of complaining.

RULE 1. *Make sure the complaint is valid.* The plant you bought your mother for her birthday is dying. Are you sure you followed the watering directions? Your new calculator does not work properly. Could that be because it dropped from the top of your dresser? If the fault is really yours, don't bother the manufacturer or merchant about the problem.

RULE 2. *If you have a complaint on a recent purchase, go back to the store immediately.* Since merchants rely on goodwill for continued business, most stores will want you to go away happy. When you go to the store to complain, be sure to deal with the person who has the authority to satisfy you. Talk to a manager, not just a salesperson. If the store has a complaint-handling procedure, such as a customer-service department, be sure to use it.

RULE 3. *If complaining to the store doesn't bring results, go straight to the top.* Address your letter to the president of the company. Although the president will refer your complaint to lower-level staff, the staff member assigned to look into your problem will be less inclined to bury your letter when it has been referred by the top boss.

Avoid addressing a letter as follows:

Funtime Video, Inc.
1111 Film Street
Los Angeles, California 90069

Dear Sir or Madam:

A letter addressed this way could float around an office for weeks until it reaches the right desk. Instead of ending up with the appropriate person, its final destination could be the wastebasket. Address your letter this way instead:

Ms. Ellen Jones
President
Funtime Video, Inc.
1111 Film Street
Los Angeles, California 90069

Dear Ms. Jones:

This letter has a much better chance of being channeled to the appropriate person. Frequently, consumers don't address their correspondence to any specific person because they don't know who is in charge. This information is not difficult to ascertain. You can obtain the names of the top executives of most major corporations, along with company addresses, in the Standard and Poor's reference books in your library.

RULE 4. *Be specific as to what the problem is and what action you want taken to resolve it.* Decide whether you want a refund, exchange, or repairs on defective merchandise. Even if you don't get what you request, it puts you and the company at a good starting point. Whatever you do, don't write a letter like this one:

June 10, 19——

Mr. John Jacobs
President
Ace Camera Company
2222 Photo Road
Albany, New York 12260

Dear Mr. Jacobs:

My new Ace camera doesn't work. I only bought it two weeks ago, and I've had problems since the first time I used it. I hope you will do something about this defective product. I look forward to hearing from you soon.

Very truly yours,
Donald Luckett

This letter doesn't say what is wrong with the camera. A company cannot begin to satisfy a consumer without knowing the specific problem. The letter also omits how the customer would like to see the situation resolved. Stating what action should be taken speeds up the time it takes to handle a complaint. Try writing a letter like this instead:

June 10, 19——

Mr. John Jacobs
President
Ace Camera Company
2222 Photo Road
Albany, New York 12260

Dear Mr. Jacobs:
The shutter on my Ace camera (model #235) sticks. I bought this camera at your Oswego store on May 2 of this year, and the shutter has been like this from the first time I used it. I would like to exchange this item for a new camera of the same make and model. I was away on vacation and so I was unable to complain to the store manager at Oswego until yesterday. Since more than four weeks has gone by, the manager, Mr. Dill, said I'd have to write to you directly. Enclosed is a copy of my sales receipt. I look forward to your reply, and I will wait three weeks before seeking third-party assistance.

Very truly yours,
Donald Luckett

This letter tells the problem and asks for specific action. It makes it easier for the company to handle the complaint and thus increases the customer's chances of a satisfactory reply.

RULE 5. *Include all necessary details.* Omitting facts will only delay action. Make sure your letter includes the make and model number of the product, the price you paid, the name and location of the store where you bought the merchandise, and the date(s) of purchase and of all previous correspondence. Don't write a letter such as this:

September 9, 19——

Ms. Jane Hobbins
Vice President, Customer Relations
Lalo Clothing
Walnut Drive
Newark, New Jersey 07101

Dear Ms. Hobbins:
I just bought one of your blouses on sale. I washed it, following the directions carefully, but it shrank. I complained to the store, but the manager said they didn't give refunds on sale items. Since the product is defective, I think you should return my money.

Sincerely,
Tracy Allen

This letter omits important facts. It doesn't identify the blouse. The manufacturer can't do anything for the customer without knowing which make of blouse is involved. Before this complaint can be resolved, the consumer must be contacted for more details. To avoid this type of delay, write a letter like this one:

September 9, 19——

Ms. Jane Hobbins
Vice President, Customer Relations
Lalo Clothing
Walnut Drive
Newark, New Jersey 07101

Dear Ms. Hobbins:

On August 20, I bought a blue Clavel brand blouse, stock #321, from the Emporium Department Store in Morristown, New Jersey. One week later, I washed the blouse. Although I carefully followed the washing instructions, the blouse shrank.

On September 1, I spoke with Mrs. Tuff, the store manager at the Emporium. Since she informed me that the store does not give refunds on sale items, I'm writing to you to request my money back. Enclosed is a copy of my receipt and the washing instructions. I look forward to hearing from you, and I will wait three weeks before seeking third-party assistance.

Sincerely,
Tracy Allen

This letter is factual and to the point. The manufacturer will not have to contact the consumer for additional information. This means that a decision concerning a refund can be made without delay.

RULE 6. *Make sure your letter takes the right tone.* Avoid sounding too apologetic or too angry. Never use personal criticism or threats. Although you may be tempted to write a poison-pen letter to a company, don't do it. All you'll succeed in doing is getting your letter thrown in the "crank" pile. Avoid sending a letter such as this:

October 1, 19——

Mr. J. Barnett
Barnett Record Stores, Inc.
44 Lansing Lane
Boulder, Colorado 80306

Dear Creep:
Your records are as warped as your mind. I just bought a Hilo Trio jazz album, and it is the worst I've ever heard. My baby brother's crying sounds better than this record. You just want to cheat the public with your lousy product. I hope you go out of business.

Thanks for nothing,
Jack Morton

Most companies would not bother to respond to this letter. Since the person reading your complaint probably has not dealt with you before, it's important that your letter make a good first impression. Not only should you avoid personal attacks, but you must also make reasonable requests. Do not make ridiculous demands such as in the letter that follows:

October 1, 19———

Mr. J. Barnett
Barnett Record Stores, Inc.
44 Lansing Lane
Boulder, Colorado 80306

Dear Mr. Barnett:

On September 15, I bought a Hilo Trio jazz album from your store in Denver. I especially wanted it for a party I was having that evening. When I played the record, it sounded terrible. The album was warped. Since I was planning on playing the record at my party, I want you to replace the album and send me money to hold another party.

Very truly yours,
Jack Morton

Jack's complaint is legitimate, but his demand is not. The company is not going to send him money for another party, and he may have ruined his chances of getting the album replaced. If your demand is unreasonable, the company may not take your letter seriously. Don't write a letter that is angry or sarcastic, or makes outlandish requests. You'll get better results if you're firm but polite. Send a letter like this one:

October 1, 19———

Mr. J. Barnett
Barnett Record Stores, Inc.
44 Lansing Lane
Boulder, Colorado 80306

Dear Mr. Barnett:
I bought a Hilo Trio jazz album from your store in Denver on September 15. As soon as I arrived home, I played the record on my stereo and discovered that it was warped. The sound was horrible. The next day I went back to the store and spoke to the manager, Mr. Hill. He offered me an exchange, but there weren't any Hilo Trio albums left. Since I didn't want any other record, I requested my money back. Mr. Hill told me that I'd have to contact you for a refund. Enclosed is a copy of my sales receipt, which states the price that I paid. I think you should reimburse me for this amount.

I am looking forward to your reply, and I will wait three weeks before I contact my local department of consumer affairs.

Very truly yours,
Jack Morton

This letter is much more effective than the other two. It's businesslike, and tells what happened and what action the consumer wants taken. (Note: To make sure you create a good impression, check your spelling, grammar, and punctuation. A poorly written letter will lose respect.)

RULE 7. *Include documents to substantiate your complaint, such as sales receipts, warranties, or newspaper ads.* Never mail originals; they could get lost. Send copies instead.

RULE 8. *Be sure to include your name and ad-*

dress in the body of the letter. It's not enough to have your return address on the envelope, since the envelope is often thrown away.

RULE 9. *Allow three weeks for the office to review your complaint.* Mention that if you don't hear from them in that period of time, you'll seek outside help.

RULE 10. *If you're not satisfied with a company's response, or if you get no response at all, contact your local consumer-affairs agency.* If there is no such agency in your city or county, write to the state office that deals with consumer problems. Some states have a separate department of consumer affairs, while others handle consumer matters out of the attorney general's or governor's office. If you're not sure where to turn for help, contact one of your local elected officials. They are familiar with government and should know where to refer your complaint.

You can decrease the chances of problems if you use common sense and good judgment. Don't let greed or laziness draw you into consumer traps. Investigate products thoroughly, read labels and warranties carefully, and deal only with reputable companies. Remember, however, no matter how carefully you shop, you will occasionally get stuck with defective merchandise or poor service. When a problem does arise, don't sit back and take it—or be taken. Follow the rules for effective complaining and you will get results.

Index

DATE DUE

FEB 0 6 2012

The Library Store #47-0119